WINTER
Tales

Illustrated by Alison Edgson

KT-362-469

Newport Community Learning
and Libraries

Z640162

WINTER
Tales

STRIPES PUBLISHING
An imprint of Magi Publications
1 The Coda Centre, 189 Munster Road, London SW6 6AW

A paperback original
First published in Great Britain in 2008

This collection copyright © Stripes Publishing, 2008
Stories copyright © Michael Broad, Julia Green,
Holly Webb, Caroline Pitcher, Malachy Doyle,
Karen Wallace, Elizabeth Baguley, Penny Dolan 2008
Illustrations copyright © Alison Edgson, 2008

The right of Alison Edgson to be identified as the
illustrator of this work has been asserted by her in accordance
with the Copyright, Designs and Patents Act, 1988.

ISBN: 978-1-84715-069-1

All rights reserved.

This book is sold subject to the condition that it shall not, by way of
trade or otherwise, be lent, resold, hired out, or otherwise circulated
without the publisher's prior consent in any form of binding or cover
other than that in which it is published and without a similar condition,
including this condition, being imposed upon the subsequent purchaser.

A CIP catalogue record for this book is available from the British Library.

Printed and bound in Belgium.

2 4 6 8 10 9 7 5 3

Contents

THE COOLEST
POLAR BEAR

Michael Broad

My name is Arthur and I am a polar bear cub. I live in the North Pole with my mum and loads of other animals, like foxes and seals and wolves and hares. The North Pole is at the top of the world, and of all the animals living here I think polar bears are the coolest.

Us polar bears live in snowy burrows and can swim in the icy ocean because we have very thick fur to keep us warm. We are completely white except for our black noses, and if we don't want to be seen in the snow, we can put a paw on our nose and become invisible!

The North Pole is not just home to animals. There's also a man who lives here with lots of elves and some reindeer. Unlike polar bears, he is very easy to spot in the snow because he always wears red and jingles when he walks. The man's name is Santa Claus.

One morning, when I was going out to play, Mum told me that I should not bother the man in red today. She explained that it was

Christmas Eve, and that he would be very busy making wishes come true for children all around the world.

"How does he make wishes come true?" I asked.

"I have no idea," said Mum. "Christmas is for humans and has nothing to do with us."

Now polar bears are very curious animals, and I thought that making wishes come true would be very interesting to see. So I put a paw on my nose and went over the hill to see Santa and his elves and his reindeer. Mum only said that I should not *bother* him, but because

I was invisible no one saw me peeping through the window of his workshop.

Santa Claus was busy reading letters from a sack and making lists, which was a bit boring to watch. The elves were busy wrapping up toys and writing labels, which was not very exciting either. The reindeer were busy munching loudly on turnips. So no one heard me trudge back home with a disappointed sigh.

Making wishes come true is not as interesting as it sounds.

Back over the hill there seemed to be something *very* interesting happening, though, because all the local animals were gathered at the edge of the ice. I ran up to my mum and asked her what was going on.

"There you are, Arthur!" she said excitedly. "You're just in time for the penguins!"

"What's a penguin?" I asked, because I didn't know.

"Penguins are birds that live in the South Pole," Mum explained. "The South Pole is on the other side of the world, but they come here once a year on holiday. They're always a lot of fun to watch."

When Mum said penguins were

birds, I looked up in the sky, but I couldn't see anything. I asked if penguins were sky-coloured with black beaks, so that when they put a wing over their beak they become invisible.

"No, darling." Mum chuckled, and pointed out towards the ocean.

It was then that I saw my first penguin, followed by another and another. Soon there were loads of penguins coming over the horizon, leaping into the air, then diving back into the waves as they swam towards us.

When they reached the ice, the penguins shot out of the water like

black and white acrobats, landing
upright in the snow, and then
flapping the water from their
flippers. Everyone cheered and
welcomed the penguins back to the
North Pole, but I was too amazed
to say anything.

Mum explained that the penguins
like to come to the North Pole
because the slopes are smoother
than in the South Pole, and that
penguins like nothing more than
snow-surfing.

"What's snow-surfing?" I asked.

"You'll see," Mum said, as the
strange new visitors waddled up
the hill.

The penguins put on an amazing show for everyone, zooming down the slopes on their bellies and sideways on their feet. And when they hit the edge of the ice they did back-flips and front-flips, before splashing into the ocean.

It was then that I decided penguins were even *cooler* than polar bears!

When the show was over, I waited until the other animals went home, and then asked the penguins if they could teach me how to snow-surf. They were very friendly, and showed me how to take a good run up and launch on to my belly.

But no matter how hard I tried, I was much too big and furry to move very fast. I had to kick my legs the whole way down the slope, and by the time I reached the edge of the ice I just plopped into the water.

I tried for hours and hours, but I still couldn't snow-surf. Then Mum called me in for my dinner, so I said goodbye to my new friends and plodded home feeling very unhappy.

"What's the matter, darling?" Mum asked. "You've hardly touched your fish."

"I wish I was a penguin," I said. "Penguins are *much* cooler than polar bears!"

"I'm afraid polar bears can't become penguins, Arthur."

"I suppose not," I sighed.

I went to bed early that night, but I couldn't get to sleep. I kept thinking about the penguins and how brilliant it must be to surf on the snow. Then I remembered that it was still Christmas Eve, the night that Santa Claus granted wishes!

Mum had said that this special night was just for human children, but I was sure Santa wouldn't mind granting a wish for one little polar bear cub. So I crept out of bed, left the burrow and set off for his workshop.

The Northern Lights lit up the sky in waves of pink and green, as I made my way across the snow. When I reached the top of the hill, I saw the reindeer tethered to a large sleigh outside Santa's workshop. The sleigh was filled with parcels, and Santa Claus was climbing into his seat at the front!

I bounded down the hill as fast as I could, as Santa took the reins and the reindeer eagerly shook their antlers. I even called out to him, but he couldn't hear me over the sound of sleigh-bells ringing in the air.

I knew the only way I'd reach the sleigh in time was if I surfed like a penguin, so I launched myself belly first on to the snow. But my legs got in the way and I tumbled head-over-tail down the slope, and

when I finally rolled to a stop I was
a great big snowball!

I quickly shook off the snow to
find I was alone.

Looking up, I could see Santa's
sleigh flying through the night sky,
soaring through the Northern
Lights with silver stars twinkling in
its path.

It was a wonderful sight, but it meant I couldn't tell Santa my wish.

"Christmas is for human children and has nothing to do with polar bears," I sighed.

I was about to go home again when I realized that none of the human children had come to the North Pole to tell Santa their wishes. Which meant the letters I'd seen him reading must have been from them!

So before I left, I crept into the workshop and wrote Santa a letter myself.

Dear Santa Claus,
I am a polar bear
and I wish I was a penguin.
Can you make my wish come
true?
Thank you,
Arthur
P.S. I hope you don't mind that
I used your paper and pencil.

The next morning I leaped out of bed feeling very excited to begin my first day as a penguin. But when I looked down I saw a white, fluffy belly and white, furry legs, and I

still had paws and not flippers.
I lifted a paw to my face, but
instead of a beak I found a familiar
black nose.

"Polar bears can't become
penguins," I sighed.

"Arthur!" Mum called from
outside our burrow. "Arthur, come
quick!"

When I climbed outside, Mum
was standing beside a tall, red
parcel and she was scratching her
head. The penguins were gathered
around, too, and they all looked just
as bewildered.

"It says *To Arthur the Polar Bear*
on the label," Mum gasped.

I stepped up to the parcel and tore off a small piece of paper, followed by another and another. Then, being a curious polar bear, I couldn't help ripping the rest away in one go. But when the parcel was unwrapped I still didn't know what it was until the penguins began clapping their flippers excitedly.

"What is it?" I asked, peering up at the tall, blue object sticking out of the snow.

"It's a surfboard!" cheered the penguins.

I'd never seen a surfboard before, but it didn't take long for me to work out how to use it. And with

the help of the penguins, I spent the
whole of Christmas Day zooming
down the slopes!

I started off on my belly,
and then
learned how
to stand up
sideways, and I
even learned how to
do front-flips and back-
flips into the ocean!

Being a polar bear was pretty
cool again, and being a polar bear
with a surfboard was even cooler.
I still think penguins are amazingly
cool, but the coolest of all is
definitely Santa Claus!

REINDEER GIRL

Julia Green

Inga stared out of the window into the snowy darkness. "When will Papa get back?" she called to her mum.

"He won't be long, now!" Mum came to the kitchen doorway. Her face was red and hot from the stove. "Come and help me make Christmas biscuits."

Inga climbed down from the window seat. She was fed up with waiting and watching for Papa to come home. He had gone to fetch Grandma for Christmas. He should have been back hours ago.

It was only the early afternoon, but in the middle of winter, in the Arctic North, it is dark all day as well as all night. Inga was used to it, just as she was used to it being light all day and all night in the summer time. In the spring and summer months, Inga made the long journey with her family and their reindeer herds to the islands off the coast. In the winter months, they lived in their snug little house on the outskirts of the town.

The house was close to the

forest, where the reindeer herd grazed on the moss and lichen underneath the soft snow. On days like today, when the snow and ice froze solid, the reindeer couldn't reach the lichen and moss, so Inga and her father took hay for them to eat.

Inga rolled out the biscuit dough. She cut out stars and heart shapes and put them carefully on the baking tray.

Mum slid the tray into the hot oven. "When they are cooked, we will thread them with ribbon, and hang them on the birch branch," she said.

Inga and Mum made paper snowflakes next, to hang up for Christmas decorations. Baby Lars watched Inga. He cooed and chirruped and waved his star-shaped hands. Everything was ready for Christmas now. Mum put candles on the table, ready for the special Christmas Eve supper.

Inga went to the window again. Still Papa and Grandma didn't come! The wind howled and whistled round the house, like a wolf trying to get in. But it couldn't. Inga was glad the walls and windows were so

tight and solid. Not like the summer
tents, the lavvu, that they lived in
during their long journey in the
summer time.

Inga held baby Lars up so he
could see out of the window, too.
He pointed at
the long icicles
hanging down
from the roof
and laughed. It
began to snow
again, small icy
flakes that made
a pebbly noise
against the
window glass.

"I can't think what's taking them so long!" Mum said. She stirred the reindeer stew on the stove, ready for supper. "If Papa isn't back soon, you will have to take the hay to the reindeer by yourself today, Inga."

Mum helped Inga pull on her fur-lined reindeer-skin boots, and her fur coat with a big collar, and her fur hat with ear flaps. Finally, Inga put on the beautiful red mittens that Grandma had made for her last Christmas. She was snug and ready for work! Inga had helped look after the reindeer herd ever since she was a tiny girl. She even had four reindeer of her own, each with a special mark cut into its ear.

Mum picked up Lars and opened the door for Inga. She handed her a big, warm shawl, to wrap round her in the sledge. Inga walked the short distance to the barn. She turned to wave, and Mum went back into the house. It was too cold outside for baby Lars today.

Inside the barn it smelled of sweet, dry hay and the strong scent of animals. They kept the tame reindeer in the barn, ready to pull the sledges or for riding. The reindeer stamped their hooves on the barn floor, and jostled their big antlers. They pushed forwards their soft brown muzzles for Inga to stroke them.

"Hello, Sky," Inga said to her favourite reindeer. She patted Sky's rough, furry neck and scratched the creamy fur on her head between her antlers. Sky liked that.

Inga put the harness round Sky's neck and filled the sledge with hay. She hitched Sky up to the sledge, and led her out of the barn. Inga knew exactly what to do, she had helped Papa so many times. Inga was proud of knowing all the Sami ways of working with reindeer.

"Let's go!" Inga shook the reins and Sky started to trot. Sky's job was to take her to the place in the forest where the herd was sheltering. Sky knew just where to go. Her hooves gripped perfectly, and the sledge runners slid easily over the fresh snow.

Inga heard the reindeer before she could see them in the darkness. They were like a heaving sea, pawing at the snow and snorting and rattling their antlers with each other. They were hungry.

"Whoa, Sky!" Inga pulled on the reins and Sky stopped and lowered her head, so the bells on the harness jingled.

The reindeer crowded round as Inga scattered armfuls of hay for them. They pulled at it with their soft mouths.

"There! All done!" Inga climbed back on to the sledge. "Home again, Sky!"

It was snowing again. Inga pulled her hat down and wrapped the shawl tight round her face, just leaving a space for her eyes. The wind was freezing.

She thought about Papa for the millionth time that day. Perhaps he was taking so long because something had happened. What if Grandma was ill? Or Papa had run out of fuel for the snowmobile? Perhaps they were stuck somewhere, broken down?

"Let's go and look for Papa," Inga said out loud. "Go to Grandma's house, Sky."

The reindeer slowed to a walk.

Her ears twitched, as if she was listening.

In the distance, Inga could see the lights of the town. They were almost home. She pulled sharply on the rein in her right hand, to make Sky turn in the other direction.

Sky trotted faster again. She understood. She had been to Grandma's house many times before.

The snow fell faster. It was so cold, so dark. Inga's toes were snug in her fur-lined boots, but her fingers were cold, her nose was like ice, her eyes stung. The wind seemed stronger and wilder, tugging

at her. Inga started to feel scared.
What if she was going in the wrong
direction? What if Sky was taking
her out on to the snowy plains, in
the middle of nowhere? The air was
full of white, swirling snow-feathers.

Inga felt sleepy, sitting still while
Sky pulled the sledge along. She
knew she must not fall asleep in the
cold. She clapped her hands together
to warm them up. She started to
sing one of the songs that Grandma
had taught her, a song to the snow:

*"The snow is cold, but also a
blanket..."*

She sang another song for Sky,
her special reindeer:

"Swift and strong, you run all day
In the thickest blizzard you find
the way..."

Singing out loud in the middle of the blizzard made Inga feel stronger and braver. She sang as loud as she could.

And suddenly Inga heard something else, besides the soft thud thud of Sky's hooves and the swish of the sledge runners and the whistle of the wind. Another voice was singing out the exact same words as Inga!

"The snow is cold, but also a
blanket..."

Inga's heart beat faster. She knew

that voice! It was Grandma's! She strained forwards, peering through the snow and the darkness. Was that a light ahead?

Sky's pace slowed down. Her ears pricked up.

"Inga?" Papa's voice! "What on earth are you doing here?"

"I heard your song," Grandma said. "What a lovely surprise!"

"What happened to you?" Inga asked. She climbed down from the sledge.

Papa hugged her tight. "I drove the snowmobile right into a big drift, by mistake. We got well and truly stuck. I tried shovelling the snow, but I still couldn't shift it. Now you are here, we can hitch up a rope to the reindeer and pull the snowmobile out. Poor Grandma's got very cold."

"Rubbish!" Grandma said. "I'm fine. But didn't I always say, Inga, that the old ways are the best? A reindeer would never get stuck in snow like that silly machine! New technology? Hah!"

Papa laughed. He heaved and shoved the snowmobile, and Inga and Grandma helped, and Sky pulled the rope, and little by little, together they freed it from the snowdrift.

Grandma
tucked
herself under
her special fur
rug in the sledge.
Inga gave Sky a handful
of hay to eat, and then climbed
up and snuggled next to Grandma
under the rug. She picked up the
reins and they began the journey
home. Papa followed behind on
the snowmobile.

At last, Inga saw the faint lights of
the town in the distance, and then
the light from the windows of their

own house, shining out over the snow. There was the barn!

Mum was already opening the door, running out to hug Inga and hold her tight. "I was worried!" she said.

Grandma told her what had happened. "Inga and Sky came to the rescue," she said. "I don't know what we'd have done without them."

Papa helped Inga to unhitch the sledge. Inga led Sky back into the barn. She fed her dried lichen, and rubbed the creamy fur on her head.

Sky looked as tired as Inga felt!

Inside the warm house, Mum helped Inga pull off her boots, and her coat and hat and mittens. Lars gurgled and waved his little hands. The candles on the table shone bright.

"Supper's ready! Sit up at the table, everyone!" Mum ladled hot, spicy reindeer stew into bowls.

Papa thanked the reindeer spirits for the precious gifts of food and family.

Grandma smiled at Inga. "And a special thank you to Sky and Inga," she said.

Inga looked at everyone round the table: Grandma and Papa and Mum and Lars, all happy and smiling and warm in the little winter house.

She looked at the paper snowflakes hanging from the birch branches in the corner of the room, and the piles of presents underneath.

Outside was the snow blizzard and the cold and darkness, but inside all was snug and cosy and safe.

"Now," Grandma said, "time for a story, and a song, and then off to bed. Tomorrow it will be Christmas Day!"

But before Inga had heard more than the first words of the story, she was already drifting asleep...

"Once upon a time, a reindeer girl was staring out into the snowy darkness..."

MIA AND
THE LOST
PENGUIN

Holly Webb

"I'm so sorry you can't come, Mia."
Mum tucked the duvet round me
gently. "Dad will look after you,
though. Just call if you need
anything, won't you?"

I made a gaspy, rattling noise –
that was all I could manage at the
moment.

"Well, just thump on the floor,
and he'll hear that." Mum looked
down at me worriedly, but then my
big sister Sophie yelled up the stairs.

"Mum, we'll be late! The theatre won't let us in if we're not there on time!" Mum gave me an apologetic smile and hurried out, leaving me sniffing miserably.

It was so unfair. It was Christmas Eve, and I had the world's worst cold, and I was missing our special Christmas treat, going to see *The Nutcracker*. I love ballet, and I'd been looking forward to it for ages. But I couldn't really sit in the theatre coughing and blowing my nose and putting everybody off the wonderful story and the dancing and the costumes – oh, it was just so unfair!

Mum had said to try and sleep, but I didn't feel tired. She'd left loads of new books from the library, and Sophie had even lent me the TV from her bedroom, but I didn't feel like that either.
I was too miserable. I flumped over on to my side, grumbling as I coughed again, and hugged Ferdie, my old toy penguin. I've had him since I was about two, and he's my best thing. I love penguins, I have loads of posters of them, and I was wearing my blue, fluffy penguin pyjamas.

"You all right, Mia?" Dad popped his head round the door.

"It's started to snow, look! We're going to have a white Christmas!"

I wriggled up on to my elbow and peered across to the window. He was right. Fat, lazy snowflakes were floating down against a dark-grey sky. It had been so cold that the snow was bound to settle as well. Great. All my friends would be out making snowmen on Christmas Day, and I'd be stuck inside, if Mum even let me get out of bed.

As I lay there dreamily watching the whirling snowflakes, with Ferdie tucked under my arm, it got colder and colder. At first I thought it was just because I could see the snow falling and it was making me feel cold, but then I realized I could see my breath puffing out in front of me. I sat up, pulling my duvet round my shoulders like a big, warm cloak.

Then, suddenly, Ferdie wriggled under my arm, his grey feathers silky-soft. I looked down in amazement, and he gazed back shyly with his bright, beady eyes, his head on one side. Then he wriggled out of the duvet, and hopped clumsily down on to the snow, still looking back at me as though he wasn't quite sure what I was.

I shook myself, trying to wake up.

I had to be dreaming. I still had my blue penguin pyjamas on, and I was all wrapped up in my duvet, but my bedroom had disappeared. Instead, I was in the middle of a snowfield, surrounded by white, as far as I could see.

I stared around me, blinking at the brightness of the shining snow. The wind was shrieking in my ears, and flurries of snowflakes swirled around me, making me shiver. It looked as though a storm was just blowing over. I glanced over my shoulder, and gasped – huge, snow-covered mountains were rising behind us, back where I'd stupidly

thought my bedroom would be
waiting. I shook my head slowly,
and took a deep breath of freezing
cold air. Meanwhile, Ferdie was
waddling clumsily away across
the whiteness.

"Hey! Stop!" I jumped up, not wanting to lose the only thing I knew in this strange world, and Ferdie looked back at me hopefully. He waggled his flipper, as if to tell me to hurry up, and carried on lurching across the hard-packed snow. I followed him, skidding and sliding, and tripping over my duvet.

"This has to be a dream," I murmured, looking down at my bare feet stepping over the Antarctic snow. "If it was real, my feet would have probably turned blue and fallen off by now..."

Ferdie seemed anxious. It was clear that he wasn't just going for

a walk, he was trying to get
somewhere. He was only a chick,
and he shouldn't really be out on his
own – he should be with his parents
or the other penguin chicks. I guessed
he must have wandered away in the
snowstorm, and got lost.

He was hopping and bouncing
over the bumpy ground, flapping his
funny little flippers for balance. But
he didn't seem to be very good at it;
he kept falling over, even though his
little black feet had sharp claws to
help him grip. I couldn't help
giggling; he looked so funny. He
was so fat and furry, with his little
black and white head bobbing about

on top of his grey, fluffy body.

But after the third fall, I stopped laughing, or even wanting to. Ferdie could hardly get up. He seemed so tired, and he just lay down in the snow. His bright, beady eyes looked back at me sadly, and then he closed them, and he didn't move.

I caught up with Ferdie, and crouched down beside him. "Ferdie! Ferdie, wake up! You can't sleep here!" I looked round worriedly. "You'll freeze." *I* was cold, and I was only a dream-person, not even really there. Ferdie might have all that gorgeous fluff, but I was pretty sure it wouldn't keep him warm for very long, if he just lay there in the snow.

Ferdie's eyes flickered open for a moment, and he gave a sad little sigh, but then they closed again. They hadn't been as bright and shiny this time; they were starting to look misted over. Ferdie was giving up.

Gently I reached out to stroke him. I cuddled my toy Ferdie all the time, but this Ferdie was real, and he was wild. I didn't want to scare him. Ferdie hardly even moved when I brushed his soft feathers with my hand. Tears dripped out of the corners of my eyes, and I felt them freezing on my cheeks.

"Don't give up, Ferdie, please!"

I whispered. And, hoping that I wasn't doing the wrong thing, I scooped him up in my arms. He was a lot heavier than my toy penguin, and bigger. He smelled like fish. He wriggled a little, as though he didn't think someone should be cuddling him, but then he didn't move.

Clumsily, dragging the duvet still – I didn't want to let go of it, it felt like my only bit of home – I trailed on. Ferdie had been following a straight path. If I looked back, I could see the marks of his shuffling feet – although I hadn't left any footprints at all, I suppose dream-people don't. So I tried to carry on going in the same sort of line. Ferdie seemed to get heavier with every step I took.

At last, we came to a little rise in the snowfield, and I dragged my way slowly up it. Then I gasped. Stretched out on the ice in front of me were thousands and thousands of penguins. They were emperor penguins, I could tell because they had black heads with orange patches on the sides. That strange noise I had thought was the wind was the penguins calling to each other, loud sounds, almost like a donkey braying.

I was so excited to see them that I accidentally hugged Ferdie tight, and he made a funny little cross noise. At least he was waking up a bit; it must have been me cuddling him and making him warm again.

Then I had a horrible thought. This was Ferdie's home, but there were at least two thousand penguins here! Which ones did he belong to? "Oh, Ferdie," I muttered to the fluffy bundle tucked inside my duvet. "I'm sure this is where you wanted to get to. But I don't know how you're going to find your mum or dad."

Ferdie was wriggling now, then he popped his little black head out of my duvet and stared round eagerly, his eyes bright and alert. He tried to flap his flippers, and I guessed he wanted to get down, so I placed him gently on the ice, wondering sadly what he was going to do. The penguins all looked alike to me, and there were hundreds of other fluffy grey chicks, too.

Ferdie waddled down the little slope determinedly, and started to rock his head backwards and forwards, calling loudly. I could only just hear him, though, because all the other chicks were doing the

same, shouting, "Piu! Piu!" again
and again, louder and louder every
time, and their parents were hastily
trying to feed them.

I looked around, wondering if any
of the other penguins would be kind
enough to give Ferdie some food, but
they were all looking after
their own chicks. Poor
Ferdie, he'd come so
far, but he was still
all alone.

Then, suddenly,
an enormous
penguin barged
past me, heading
straight for Ferdie.

He was one of the tallest ones I'd seen, he was right up to my waist, and he nearly knocked me over. He *did* knock Ferdie over, but obviously because he was so delighted to see his lost chick. He nudged him up at once, snuggled him into his tummy feathers and started feeding him.

I was colder again without Ferdie to cuddle, so I sat down to wrap myself in my duvet. It was so cold I began to feel sleepy. The snow was falling again, those same great fat flakes there'd been outside my window at home. I wondered how I was going to get back there. *But at least I rescued Ferdie,* I thought.

He's home safe...

"Hey, Mia... Time for your medicine, sweetheart." Dad was sitting on my bed, gently shaking me. "Wow, it's chilly in here. I'd better turn the radiator up."

I blinked at him. Surely seconds ago I'd been in a snowfield full of penguins?

"Were you dreaming, Mia? You look a bit dazed." Dad smiled at me as he poured the medicine.

"Mmm." I took a quick look around. This was definitely my room.

And there was Ferdie, on my pillow. Fluffy and snuggly, smiling and safe...

TWO LITTLE
SNOW
LEOPARDS

Caroline Pitcher

In a mountain cave in the land of
Tibet lived two little snow leopards
with their mother. Their names
were Meru and Maya.

Maya rolled over and waved her
big paws in the air. Underneath they
were thick with fur.

"Why are my feet so big and
furry, Mum?" she cried.

"To help you walk in the deep
snow and to protect your paws
from the cold," said her mother.

"If you think your paws are big, just look at mine."

"Wow!" squealed the cubs.

Their mother laughed. "Our furry feet are our snowshoes, my beautiful cubs."

"Your tummy is furry, too, Maya," said Meru. "You've got a big, furry belly." He batted her ear with his big paw. "Mum's eyes are iced-gold, but yours are sky-blue."

Maya squeaked. "You've got sky-blue eyes and thick fur, too, you know, Meru. All furry-blurry! All white, with spots and rings. And it looks like snow-clouds are floating across your back."

Their mother looked down at them and said, "Your thick fur will keep you warm. It is pale and dark like the snow and rocks. The mountainside is a snow-leopard landscape and your fur will make you invisible. No one can see you out there. You are two little secrets in the snow."

"Good!" said Meru.

"We're invisible!" squeaked Maya.

She swiped at Meru, and the cubs tussled and tumbled, until their mother growled softly. "Stop that now," she said. "Let's sleep. I'm going hunting at dawn, and won't be back until nightfall."

"Can we come, too?" chorused the cubs.

"No. I shall go alone," she said. "You are still too small."

"Can we play outside while you're away?"

"Yes. But don't stray too far from the cave. Always be sure you can see the juniper tree that grows outside. Then you won't get lost."

"Silly old juniper tree!" sniffed Meru. "It's just a big stick with prickles and a few shrivelled berries."

"It's a special juniper tree because it shows where we live," said their mother. "Now lie still and close your eyes."

Outside, the blue-black night crackled with stars. The moon tipped light down on to the mountainside. In the cave, the cubs slept safe, with their tails wrapped around them like scarves.

At dawn, the mother snow leopard looked at them once with her iced-gold eyes and slipped out of the cave alone. The cubs stirred in their sleep as her paws crunched lightly on the snow crust and she vanished into the snow-leopard landscape.

When the cubs woke, the sky was startling blue and the world was diamond bright.

"C'mon!" squeaked Meru.

"Coming!" squeaked Maya.

They scampered out of the cave and blinked in the slanting sunshine.

"Look down there," cried Meru.

"Wow!" cried Maya.

They gazed down from the mountain ledge.

A hare was nibbling at the bark of a birch tree. He stopped when he heard the cubs and disappeared down the mountainside.

Below them, Meru and Maya saw bright prayer flags snapping and flapping in the wind. In the valley, big black yaks lumbered along a track and a donkey brayed in the corral near the village.

"That looks fun. Shall we go down there?" said Meru.

"No," replied Maya. "Mum said we mustn't stray far from the cave. But look up there... Wow!"

High in the clear sky hovered a golden eagle.

As Meru looked up, Maya put her big paws round her brother's face. "C'mon! Let's play," she cried. "You pretend to be a blue mountain sheep and I'll chase you. Coming, ready or not!"

Wheee! The cubs raced up and down the mountainside, leaping from rock to rock with their tails behind them like sails, sending little avalanches sliding down the slopes to the valley.

Finally, they came to a stop and stood panting for breath, with their pink mouths open and their little sides heaving.

"Phew!" cried Meru. "I'm out of breath. We've come a really long way, Maya."

"Yes, but look at our paw prints in the snow, going all the way to our cave. And I can still see the juniper tree."

"Silly old tree," sniffed Meru. "C'mon! I'll chase you!"

They scampered off, jumping from rock to rock. They butted heads and swiped and pounced and scampered off again, until they stopped, panting. From their noses came little puffs of frozen breath.

"Look at the snow-leopard landscape," cried Maya. "The mountainside is like Mum's fur, all white with dark rings."

"Tell you what, Maya," said

Meru, "Mum said we were invisible out here, so let's play hide and seek. I'll hide first."

He trotted off and lay very still on the snow.

"Coming, ready or not..." said Maya. "Hey, Meru?"

"Yes?" he squeaked.

"Found you!" she squealed. "Now it's my turn to hide."

She scampered in and out of the rocks and hid in a crevice. Meru searched for a long time. He padded right past and did not see her. In the end he began to whimper, "It's not fair! I can't see you. Where are you, Maya?"

"Boo!" she cried, pouncing out at him. They chased around and back again.

"Hey, something dropped on my nose," squeaked Meru.

"And my head is getting wet," said Maya. "It's snowing."

"Let's toboggan!" squealed Meru, and the cubs played slipping and sliding down the mountainside.

"I can't see where I'm going now," grumbled Meru. "The snow is flying sideways. I'm tired. I think I'll have a little doze under the shelter of this rock."

"I think I will, too," yawned Maya. "I'm very sleepy."

The cubs curled up and dozed, with their tails wound around them like scarves.

While the cubs slept, the snow fell and fell, and the wind wrapped it around the mountain.

When the cubs woke up, the world was completely changed.

"Just look down there," whispered Meru. "I can't see anything at all."

"Neither can I," whispered Maya. "Maybe that big bird can show us the way back." She blinked up into the sky to find the golden eagle, but she couldn't see anything except swirling snowflakes.

"We'd better go home," she said.

"But where is home?" squeaked Meru. "I can't see the juniper tree…"

"Let's look for our paw prints," said Maya.

The cubs stared and stared, but so much snow had fallen it had covered up the trail of paw prints. Their tracks had vanished.

"Never mind," said Maya. "Let's sniff and smell where our paws have been, and follow the scent back to the cave."

The cubs sniffed and sniffed, but they could not even find the scent of their own feet. The fresh snow had hidden it.

"Oh-wuh! I want to be home and cosy inside the cave with Mum," squeaked Meru.

"At least we're invisible in this snow-leopard landscape. Nothing can get us," said Maya.

"But that means Mum won't be able to find us, either," cried Meru. "She won't be able to see us because our coats keep us a secret."

The cubs sat down. They did not know what to do. They just sat getting colder and wetter.

"You're beginning to look like a pile of snow," squeaked Maya.

"Well, I can't help it. You look like a snowball," snapped Meru.

"Don't let's squabble," said Maya. "Let's be sensible. If we fall asleep in the snow again, it will be real night-time and we will be too cold. We need to search for our juniper tree, and then we'll find home. You go that way and I'll go this way."

"No!" yowled Meru. "I'll get lost. Please let's stay together, Maya. I want to find our dear juniper tree!"

"All right," she said. "Look where we are now. You can tell we've been here from this dip in the snow. So this is our starting place... Come on, Meru."

Maya sighed and set off
across the snow,
with her
brother
trotting close
behind her.

They knew
that they must
find that juniper tree. But all they
could see was snow, falling around
them like thick feathers.

The sky was growing dark.
Soon the stars would glitter and
the mountain would be colder
than ever.

"I'm getting tired," whispered
Meru. "But I don't want to have

to sleep out here in the cold."

"Me neither," whispered Maya.

"Can you see the juniper tree yet?" said Meru.

"No," Maya said. "Can you?"

"No," he whimpered. "And I can't go any further."

"You must," she cried. "You must keep going. Soon we'll be cuddled up with Mum in our warm, dry den ... soon ... and we'll sleep so cosily... Meru?"

Behind her, Meru had stopped. His legs folded under him and he sank down in the snow.

Maya turned and sank down next to him. She nuzzled his ears

and said, "Maybe Mum will come and find us."

"She won't be able to see us in the snow-leopard landscape," insisted Meru.

"Oh dear. Cuddle up close," sighed Maya.

"All right then," he mumbled. "But I think someone has already been here and made a dip in the snow. Ow! OW!"

"What?"

"I knocked my head on something. Something prickly. It's... It's..."

"The juniper tree!" they squealed together and jumped up again.

"This is where we stopped," cried Maya. "We were next to the tree all the time and we didn't know it. We're home. And ... hello, Mum!"

"I am so proud of you both," purred their mother, as she approached the cubs. "I was going to fetch you, but I waited a moment when I saw that you were finding your own way home like big snow leopards."

"You said we were invisible!" squeaked Meru.

"You said we're two small secrets in our special fur," said Maya.

"So how could you see us out on the mountainside?" squealed Meru.

"Because I am your mother," she purred. "Now, come inside to the warmth on this cold winter's night."

Outside, the blue-black night crackled with stars. The moon tipped light down on to the mountainside. In the cave, Maya and Meru cuddled up to their mother and slept safe, with their tails wrapped around them like scarves.

MUSK

Malachy Doyle

"Wake up, child! Come and see!"

Lucy opened her eyes. There was a great hairy face, tap tap tapping with one of its long, curvy horns on her bedroom window.

Lucy blinked, not really believing what she saw. It was big, like a cow, but it definitely wasn't a cow. It was woolly, like a sheep, but it wasn't a sheep, either. It had horns, a bit like a goat, but Lucy had never seen a goat like this before.

Am I dreaming? she thought. *Is it real?*

She slid out of bed and opened the window, just a crack. A blast of icy wind hit her in the face. There was a smell, too – a strange and powerful smell.

"Hello," said Lucy. "Who are you?"

"I'm a musk ox," replied the creature. "I've come to show you something."

"I haven't heard of a musk ox," said Lucy, who'd never seen anything quite like him before, not even in the zoo. "Are you lost?"

"No, I'm not lost," replied the

musk ox. "But I've come a long way, from the frozen North – the land of snow and ice – and I need to get back as soon as I can, for it's much too warm for me here."

"Too warm?" said Lucy, shivering. "It's freezing, with the window open like that."

"Let me in, then," said the musk ox, "and I'll tell you why I've come."

So Lucy opened the window wide, just for a minute, while the animal clambered through.

"Have I come to the right place?" he asked her, trying to squeeze into the space between the bed and the wall. The room was full of him, and full of his smell, too – a strange, strong, not unpleasant smell, thought Lucy.

"Is your name Lucy?" he asked.

She nodded.

"Have you a little brother called Joe?"

She nodded again.

"You're proud of him, aren't you?" said the musk ox.

"Very," replied Lucy, who loved her little brother more than anything.

"Well, that's why I've come," said the creature.

"What do you mean?" said Lucy, confused.

"To meet you and Joe. And to show you something."

"What sort of something?"

"I can't tell you," said the musk ox. "I have to take you to see, instead. Will you come? You can ride on my back and we'll be there and home again before dawn."

"I don't know," said Lucy, frowning. "I'm not sure I should."

"It'd be lovely if you would," said the musk ox, and when Lucy glanced into his eyes, she saw stars and snow, icicles and rainbows. And she knew, just by looking at him, that she and Joe would be safe.

"All right, Mister Musk Ox," she

told him. "Wait here and I'll go and get Joe."

She threw on her dressing gown and slippers and ran to fetch her little brother. "Joe!" she cried, nudging him from sleep. "Come and see! There's the strangest animal in my bedroom, and he wants to meet you."

"Me?" Joe snuffled.

"Yes, you! He's big, like a cow," said Lucy, "with horns like a goat and all woolly, like a sheep. Come and see, Joe – quick, before he disappears!"

Joe's eyes opened wide, then, and he slid out of bed.

"He says he's going to take us on a journey through the night," Lucy whispered, helping her little brother with his dressing gown and slippers. "Here, put these on – it's cold out there. Come and see!"

She tippy-toed down the landing, with Joe padding along behind her. But suddenly he turned and rushed back to his bedroom.

"Tom..." he said, grabbing his sailor doll from the pillow. "Come, see, Tom..."

"Ah," said Lucy, smiling when she saw what he was holding. "I'd forgotten about Tom!" Joe never went anywhere without him – not even to the bathroom in the middle of the night.

Lucy led him to her room, and even though she'd told Joe what to expect, her little brother gasped when he saw the size of the great musk ox. He wrinkled up his nose, too, when he smelt him.

"Don't be frightened, Joe," said the creature. "I won't hurt you. And if you're happy to fly through the night with me, I'll make sure you come to no harm."

Joe looked at Lucy, and Lucy looked at Joe.

"We'll come, Mister Musk Ox," said Lucy, clambering over the bed to get past him to the window and open it wide.

"Hold on tight, then," said the animal, and they climbed up on to his back, grabbing hold of his woolliness.

Then, with a mighty swoosh, the musk ox flew out and over the rooftops, out and over the town.

It was the coldest of nights and there was snow all around, but the comfort of his long, brown hair kept Joe and Lucy snug. On they flew, by the light of the winter moon, over cities and farms, hills and seas, and in time the smell and the warmth of him lulled them to sleep.

"Wake up, you two," cried the musk ox, at last. "We're coming in to land!"

The children blinked and then looked all around, as they came to rest by a stable.

"Come with me, children," said the animal, leading Joe and Lucy inside.

It was dark in the stable, but there was a small light in the corner. The musk ox led them towards the light, which came from a newborn child, lying in the hay.

"Baby..." said Joe, dropping to his knees.

He whispered little Joe-words to the infant, and then remembered the sailor doll he was still clutching in his hand.

"Tom…" he said, holding it above the baby's eyes. And the newborn gurgled happily.

"Tom…" said Joe again, dangling the little sailor man by one arm and swinging him slowly from side to side.

The baby chuckled, as its eyes followed the movement.

"Baby…" said Joe, pressing the doll into the newborn's hand.

The infant clutched his tiny fingers around the precious gift, and then stared up into Joe's eyes, seeming to smile.

"But Joe…" said Lucy, shocked. "You can't give Tom away! He's your one and only! Your very best!"

"Baby…" said Joe, with a sad-little, happy-little smile. "Best baby."

The musk ox looked on, unsurprised. "You're very kind, Joe," he said, nodding his heavy head. "This child has only just been born, and you're the first person to bring him a present and welcome him into the world."

"Why is the baby's head so bright, Mister Musk Ox?" Lucy asked. "It's like he's on fire or something!"

"It's to tell everyone how special

he is," the animal answered.

"Like Joe?" said Lucy, who was ever so proud of her little Down's syndrome brother.

"Yes," said the creature. "Joe is loving and giving, just as this child will be. And now I must take you both home."

"I want you to do something for me, children," said the musk ox, as they climbed up on to his back. "I want you to tell other people you see about the baby. I want you to tell them he has come into the world. Will you do that for me?"

"We will," said Lucy. "Won't we, Joe?"

Her little brother nodded happily.

"The baby's born!" cried Lucy, as they flew through the ice-cold night. "It's Christmas morning and the baby's born!"

"Baby!" cried Joe. "Baby!"

"Where?" came a voice from far below them. "Where is this special baby you speak of? We heard that he was coming, and we have been trying to find him for days."

"In a stable," cried Lucy, pointing. "Over there!"

"Baby!" cried Joe, happily.

And the three kings, each with a gift for the newborn child, turned in the direction Lucy pointed, trudging onwards through the starlit snow.

Back in Joe and Lucy's town the Christmas bells rang out, as the musk ox helped the children into their beds.

"Where are you going, Mister Musk Ox?" asked Lucy, drowsily. He was outside the window now, pulling it shut with one of his horns.

"Home to the frozen North," whispered the great, lumbering creature. "My job is done here. Happy Christmas, Lucy."

"Happy Christmas," murmured Lucy, pulling the duvet tight around her. "Thank you for taking us to see the baby."

In the morning, when Joe and Lucy woke, there were presents at the end of their beds. And the present Joe liked best was a small wooden animal, with wool nearly to the ground, and long, curly horns.

And the one Lucy liked best was in a tiny blue box. She took off the ribbon, opened the box, and there inside was a little green bottle.

When she eased open the stopper, out came a smell that filled the whole room. It was a smell of sweetness and spice, of animal, earth and baby.

And when she looked at the label

on the front of the bottle, she
smiled at the single word that was
written there: "musk".

THE
MIDWINTER
MAGIC SHOW

Karen Wallace

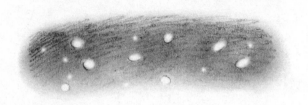

Gordon was a young grizzly bear who lived in the far, far North where winter went on for months and months. Sometimes, when the other bears were dozing or just watching the snowflakes come down, Gordon closed his eyes and dreamed his favourite dream.

Gordon's dream was to be a magician. Not just any magician. Gordon wanted to be a really good magician so that in the middle of winter, when it was coldest and darkest, he could put on a show for all the other animals and make them happy.

"Don't be daft," said Gordon's big sister Gaby. "You're a grizzly bear. You can't be a magician. You're too big and too clumsy. Besides, you don't know any tricks."

Gordon looked at his sister with his clever, bright eyes. She was the one who was big and clumsy. What's more, all she ever thought about was food. Especially in the winter when it was hard to find any. Every night in their cave, Gaby kept him awake with her sleep talking.

*Snakes, fish, frogs, birds, insects,
honey. Honey, honey, honey.*

"I can *learn* tricks," said Gordon.
"Mum will teach me."

"Don't be daft," said Gaby again.
"Mum teaches us what grizzly bears
do. Like catching fish when the ice
melts and finding moss under the
snow. What would she know about
magic tricks?"

Gaby stuffed some dry berries
left over from the summer into her
big, red mouth. "You're sthtupid,"
she said as she chomped them up.
Then she waddled away, leaving a
trail of paw prints in the snow.

Gordon stared after his sister.

Sometimes he wished she would be nice to him. Just once. But maybe that's what big sisters were like.

"Sounds as though you have a problem." A squirrel cocked his head and looked down from a branch high above Gordon.

It wasn't that the squirrel, whose name was Simon, didn't trust Gordon. They'd known each other since they were both little. But Gordon was a grizzly bear and even good friends can forget their manners sometimes.

Gordon slumped to the ground and leaned back against the trunk of the tree. A great dollop of snow fell on his head. "I want to be a magician," he said.

Simon crept a little nearer. "So what's wrong with that? You can be whatever you want."

"Gaby says I'm daft," said Gordon.

"*She's* the daft one," said Simon, firmly. "She tried to eat me yesterday! Me? How *could* she?"

"No manners and all she thinks about is food," said Gordon. "She's probably jealous of all those acorns you've got hidden in your nest." He shook the snow from his head. "Even so, she shouldn't have done that. I'll tell my mum."

"Don't bother," said Simon. "*She* tried to eat me the day before."

Gordon slumped down even further and put his head in his paws. This time he didn't bother to rub off the snow that fell on his head.

"Sorry," said Simon. "I didn't mean to make things worse. In fact, I was going to give you a tip." He tapped his head with his tiny paw. "Squirrels know a thing or two."

"What do you mean?"

"An enormous owl with eyes like yellow plates has moved into the dead tree by the big, black rock," said Simon.

"So?"

"So everyone says there's nothing that owl doesn't know," said Simon. "Thing is, Gordon, apparently he's one of those *really* wise snowy owls that come from the North Pole."

Gordon had never heard of such owls.

"Do you think he might teach me how to be a magician?" he asked.

"Why not," said Simon.

Gordon jumped up so quickly

that Simon almost fell off his branch. He always forgot how fast grizzly bears could move.

"Thanks, Simon!" cried Gordon. "You're a *real* pal!"

Ten minutes later, Gordon stood underneath the dead tree by the big, black rock. He stood up on his hind legs and scratched at the bark.

An enormous owl appeared from a hole above him. He blinked his huge, yellow eyes and shook some snowflakes off his white, feathery ears. "Bit early, isn't it?" he said.

"Sorry to disturb you," said Gordon, shyly. "But—"

"Ah yes, you're the young grizzly that wants to be a magician," interrupted Wise Owl, yawning. "Well, what can I do for you?"

Gordon was so surprised, his mouth opened but no words came out. "Can you teach me how to do magic tricks?" he said at last.

"No," replied Wise Owl. "But I do have a book you can borrow and a wand you can keep."

He disappeared into his tree and came out with a blue book under his wing and a wand in his beak. The book was called *Magic Tricks:*

The Bear Facts. He dropped them on the snow beside Gordon's feet.

"Now all you need is a cloak and top hat," said Wise Owl.

"Where will I find those?" asked Gordon.

Wise Owl hooted with laughter. "Your mother will know," he said.

Gordon ran back to where his mother was dozing in her cave. In the winter, she spent most of her time asleep.

Sure enough, Wise Owl was right. Gordon's mum muttered something about a travelling circus that had got lost in the woods many years before and terrible indigestion.

She pointed towards the back of
the cave. Under a pile of leaves, there
was an old top hat and a cloak.

For the next week, Gordon
taught himself magic tricks. Soon he
could make a bunch of flowers
appear out of his paws and pull out
shiny pebbles <u>from</u> behind his
friends' ears.

All the other animals thought he
was brilliant.

Except for his sister Gaby.

"Who wants flowers and shiny
pebbles in the middle of winter?"
Gaby took a deep breath. "We want
snakes, fish, frogs, birds, insects and
honey. Especially honey. Anyway,

you can't be a *real* magician if you don't have a rabbit."

The other animals stopped and stared. All the talk about food had made them hungry and cross.

"She's right," said an old moose.

"Can't say truer than that," growled a grey wolf.

"Gordon's not a magician! Gordon's not a magician!" squealed a white fox.

So Gordon ran back to Wise Owl's tree. He stood on his hind legs and scratched at the bark. "I need a rabbit!" he howled.

But Wise Owl wasn't there.

"Looking for someone?" A huge

great fluffy rabbit popped its head out from under the tree. At first Gordon couldn't see it because its white fur was the same colour as the snow. Also, the rabbit didn't come too close. He was a smart rabbit and his mother had always warned him about grizzly bears. *They may act sweet as pie, son, but when they're hungry, most of 'em forget their manners.*

Gordon stared at the rabbit's pink eyes and slowly made out his floppy ears and his tufty tail. He was perfect!

"Pleased to meet you," cried Gordon. "I'm a magician and I'm looking for a rabbit!"

The rabbit cocked his head. "You look like a grizzly bear to me."

"I'm a magician first and a grizzly bear second," said Gordon. He put his paw on his chest. "I promise."

The rabbit shot out from under the tree, did a full somersault and landed on the ground. "Then count me in," he cried. "I've always wanted to be a magician's rabbit."

"Haven't you forgotten something?" A skunk appeared from behind a snowy bush. "Every great magician needs a manager. Especially a good manager like me." She wrapped her bushy black and white tail around her neck like a scarf and waited. "I'll help you put on a really amazing magic show."

Gordon and the rabbit stared at each other. "What makes you such a good manager?" Gordon asked the skunk at last.

The skunk smiled a knowing smile and drew an exclamation mark in the air with the tip of her tail. "Because no one ever says no to me!"

Gordon and the rabbit turned to each other again. All the animals in the forest knew about skunks.

It was true. You didn't say no to them. Not unless you wanted to be sprayed with the worst smell in the whole world so that none of your friends would come near you again.

"OK, it's a deal," said Gordon.

The skunk chuckled. "Don't worry, you won't regret it," she said.

Weeks went by and the skunk kept her word. Soon the magic show was the talk of the forest. While Gordon and the rabbit practised amazing tricks, the skunk, whose name was Nelly, gave all the animals something to do. The moose made a huge sign.

MAGIC SHOW COMING SOON!

The other grizzly bears helped to flatten the snow to make a clearing. At first the bears all said they were too sleepy, especially Gordon's sister Gaby. But then Nelly had given them all a hard stare and swished her tail in a very dangerous way. After that, everyone did as they were told.

The night of the Midwinter Magic Show finally arrived. Wise Owl had showed the wolves and foxes how to build a stage out of ice blocks. Simon, the squirrel, had decorated it with some holly and red berries.

Gordon stood behind a huge snowy bush in his top hat and cloak. "What happens if no one likes my magic?" he asked Nelly, nervously.

Nelly smiled her knowing smile. "Just do what I say," she replied. "I have a brilliant trick for you to do." Then she whispered in his ear.

As the moon rose, the animals took their places in the clearing.

"I've heard Gordon has a brand-new trick," said a moose.

"Me too," said a deer.

"My Gordon can do *anything*," said Gordon's mum, proudly.

"Gordon is a very clever young

grizzly bear," agreed Wise Owl.

The pine tree branch curtains were pulled back and Nelly stood in the middle of the stage.

"Animals of the North!" she cried. "Welcome to our MIDWINTER MAGIC SHOW!" She stood back and held out her arms. "Now may I present Gordon the Amazing Magician!"

Suddenly, Gordon wasn't nervous any more! He made his rabbit fly out of his hat, sail over the trees and land back in his hat again. He made stars fall from the sky and juggled them like enormous diamonds. He made snow whirl around his feet like a tiny tornado.

All the animals were stunned. Not one of them had ever seen anything like it!

"And now for my last trick," cried Gordon. He smiled and turned to where Gaby was sitting at the back. "This one is especially for my sister Gaby!"

Nelly banged two heavy sticks

together on a tree stump so that
they sounded like drums.

Everyone got very excited!

What was going to happen next?

Gordon took off his cloak and
held it out in front of him. Then he
winked at Nelly and shouted,
"*Abracadabra!*"

All the animals gasped. Gaby's
eyes nearly popped out of her head.

In the middle of the stage was a
huge, long table. And it was stacked
with everyone's favourite food.
There was a mountain of moss, fish,
snakes, insects, nuts, acorns and
grass. But best of all, there was an
enormous pile of honeycombs.

Especially for Gaby!

As Gordon bowed, all the animals clapped and cheered. Then Gaby stood up and walked on to the stage. She threw her arms around Gordon's neck and gave him a great big hug.

A huge grin spread across Gordon's face. It was the first time she had ever been really nice to him.

"Three cheers for Gordon!" cried Gaby. "He is the greatest Grizzly Bear Magician in the World!"

Then, as the full moon made the black sky turn light and all around the snow sparkled like silver, the Midwinter Magic Show came to an end and the Midwinter Feast began.

The animals cheered so loudly that Gordon had to bow again. He had never felt so happy in his life.

That night, the mountain of delicious food never ran out and the feast went on and on.

Everyone
agreed that Gaby
was right.

Gordon really
was the greatest
Grizzly Bear
Magician in the World!

THE TIME
OF THE
WHITE FUR

Penny Dolan

Ookalik the hare was born when the rocky mountain was speckled with bright-green moss and tiny star-like flowers.

Ookalik and his two sisters huddled against the earth. Above them stretched the wide spring sky. Below them stretched the valley, where the larch and pine trees grew.

By night, Mother Hare warmed her young with the heat of her own body. By day, she kept watch over them. "Do not worry if I run off," Mother Hare explained. "I will not be leaving you. I will be leading away danger."

So, when Fox appeared on the mountainside, or Eagle's shadow darkened the sky, Mother Hare jumped up and ran off. Her bobbing, white tail lured enemies away from her three babies.

Before long, Mother Hare gently lifted the leverets out of their open burrow. Hop by hop, jump by jump, Ookalik and his sisters examined the world around them. In the distance, they saw other young hares playing on the mountainside.

Then, one day, Mother Hare called the three hares to her. "Listen, my little ones," she said. "You have much to learn. See that pale sun above you? It will grow into a midsummer sun. As the sun grows big and strong, so must you."

"Why?" asked little Ookalik.

"Once midsummer is over, the days grow shorter and darker. Before long, the Time of the White Fur will come. By then, you must be bold and clever enough to look after yourselves. You will be babies no more."

"The time of the White Fur?" said Ookalik. "What does that mean?"

"Silly! Don't you know? It's the time of the year when our fur turns white, of course!" his two sisters said bossily. They had been listening to other mountain hares chatting.

Ookalik stared at the speckled grey-brown fur on his back. "Will it happen soon?" he asked.

Mother Hare's eyes danced with laughter. "Not for a long time," she said. "But it is important to learn what I have to teach you before that hard time comes."

So Mother Hare set to work. She taught the three young hares how to find fresh green shoots to nibble.

She taught
them which
plants were
good to eat,
and where to
find the clearest
pools of water.

She taught them to race as fast
as the wind, too. "Your life may
depend on how fast you can run,"
she said.

She taught them the best hare
tricks: how to dart around the thorn
bushes, how to twist and turn and
double back as they ran, and how
to stay so still they would seem like
the stones around them.

"Remember," she said, "your fur is speckled grey like the rocks just now, so no enemy can see your hiding place. Then, once winter comes, your white fur will hide you while the land is white with snow."

Slowly, the sun grew warmer. It made the daytime longer. It made the night-time shorter. Young Ookalik liked the night, because he loved to stare at the full moon. He thought he could see a strange figure on the silvery disc.

"Who is that on the moon?" he asked.

"That is Moon Dancer, the greatest hare of all," Mother Hare said. She told Ookalik how the magic hare had danced so well that he had jumped right up to the moon.

I wish I could jump like Moon Dancer, Ookalik thought as he leaped about the mountain. Even when the midsummer sun came, shining all day and night, Ookalik danced, because he knew Moon Dancer was still there, hidden in the bright sky.

Then the season began to change. The sun was not so strong. The trees in the valley turned a dull, dark green. Mist came creeping over the rocks. Water filled the spaces where the flowers once peeped, and the moss turned brown.

"Beware!" Mother Hare told her children. "This is the Time of the Hunter."

One morning, men with guns stood at the foot of the hares' hill. Ookalik tried to do what his mother had done, and lure the enemies away. While his sisters crouched down by the rocks, Ookalik jumped up, and tried to dart off.

Bang! A bullet whistled past. Down dived Ookalik, into the nearest hollow. He lay there trembling, licking the place where his grey fur was torn. Sometimes it was better to hide than to be brave.

Luckily, the hunters did not come any closer. They turned and walked towards the Long Lake. All that day, the ducks and geese flew much higher in the sky.

At last a time came when the sun hardly shone. The darkness grew longer. The pools of water were crusted with ice, and it was hard to find food.

"Now you must take extra care, for there will be hungry animals about," said Mother Hare. "Especially foxes."

One afternoon, as Ookalik raced across the mountain, two strange, young hares stood in his way. Their fur seemed to be covered in white frost.

"Pleased to meet you," Ookalik said politely.

"It's only us, silly!" laughed his sisters, showing him the pale fur that lay across their backs. In a week their fur had become totally white. Ookalik stared at his own fur. It was still speckled grey.

White feathers of snow began to fall from the sky. Hour after hour they fell. The rough, rocky land was covered in soft, shining whiteness.

So this is the Time of the White Fur, Ookalik thought.

As he headed back to his burrow to find his mother, he noticed that all the other hares were covered in white fur. "Mother, what shall I do?" he asked when he reached her.

"Don't worry, Ookalik. Keep out of sight. It will happen," Mother Hare told him. "Sometimes it just takes a while."

One morning, Ookalik awoke to find the world covered in white. Now he was in great danger. Anyone could spot a grey hare moving across the white mountain. So Ookalik burrowed himself down among the drifts of snow and hid for a long time. He did not mind the dark, but he did miss seeing his hero, Moon Dancer. One night the little hare could bear it no longer. Ookalik poked his nose above the snow.

He could not see Moon Dancer, but he did see the magical lights rippling across the sky, shining red and green and blue and gold.

They flickered and gleamed, whirling and changing as if the wind itself was alight. The whole sky shimmered. Transfixed, Ookalik watched the lights dance above the wonderful whiteness of the snow.

"Grrrr! Got you, hare!" Something pounced, something with sharp teeth and a dreadful scent of blood on its rough fur. Fox!

Ookalik jumped so high that the cruel mouth snapped and missed its bite.

At once Ookalik ran, twisting this way and that way. His ears lay back. His strong feet beat on the ground. *Thump, thump, thump!*

He could feel his
own heart thudding
wildly. He could feel
the hot breath close
behind him.

"Moon
Dancer, save
me!" he cried.

Down the mountainside
raced Ookalik. Blindly, he ran into
the valley. He saw the shadowy
snow beneath the trees. Surely he
would be safer there? But Fox was
still behind him. *On, Ookalik, on!*

An old log cabin stood under the
trees. A narrow rectangle of light
appeared. Ookalik ran towards it,

darting between the feet of a man and a boy who were struggling in with a small tree. The hare pushed through the scented branches, and disappeared into the darkness beneath a cupboard. He squeezed himself into the corner, and closed his eyes in fear.

Fox was scrabbling at the metal step, but the man was shouting, using his boots and a stick to drive the enemy away. Ookalik heard a slamming sound, and realized he was trapped inside the cabin.

He shivered as a torch beam washed over him. A boy was kneeling down, peering hard.

"Something did run under here, Dad," he said, then gasped. "It's a young hare!"

"Well, the poor thing won't hurt us. It'll come out when it's good and ready," the man said. "Come on, let's get our tree set up now we've brought it home."

From his dark hiding place, Ookalik heard songs being played softly. He heard the man and boy chatting, and wrapping things in paper, and laughing. He smelt the forest scent of the tree, and the good things the man and boy were munching. Finally, the boy yawned and the father yawned.

"Bedtime!" laughed the man. The boy climbed into a bunk. The man went off to his own room

"Goodnight, little hare," said the boy.

Ookalik's night seemed to go on for ever. When all was quiet at last, he hopped out.

There in front of him stood the tree, but something had happened. The green branches were hung with round, silver balls, each one shining like a moon. Entranced, the little hare hopped closer and closer. There was something familiar about the lovely silver globes.

Then Ookalik sat up in surprise. He jumped this way and that way, his head on one side. What had he seen? There, inside each moon-like shape he saw a hare, a magical hare, dancing and swaying. It must be Moon Dancer, come to help him!

Strangely, his hero's fur was not pure white, but a soft silvery white. The little hare gazed at the tree.

Then Ookalik heard a soft noise behind him. As he turned his head and saw the young boy standing there, he also saw his own fur. Why, it had changed, too! His fur was just the same colour as Moon Dancer's!

"Hello, little hare! Happy Christmas!" the boy said. "Shall I let you out now?"

Then the boy opened the cabin door, and the winter wind outside seemed to call a name. *Ookalik!*

The little hare glanced once again

at Moon Dancer's tree; then he leaped out through the door, and danced back across the snow to where the other hares were waiting in their white, winter fur.

SEAL
BROTHER

Elizabeth Baguley

Lights shone through the Arctic darkness from the windows of a low, stone house. It was Christmas Eve, and inside, a mother was hanging the last bauble on a Christmas tree. She turned to her son, who was hugging his knees as he sat on the floor, staring at a cream-coloured disc held in his hand. In the lamplight, his pale hair looked grey and his dark eyes had the soft glimmer of ice.

"Euan! You aren't listening to me!" teased his mother. "I said, why don't you help me light the candles on the tree?" She smiled at him. He hadn't heard her asking him about the lights. His mind wasn't on the tree with its winking tinsel. He was thinking about the sea, as always.

Euan held the cream disc tightly. It was a whalebone on which Father had carved a picture of his fishing boat, *The Midnight Sun*. When Father went away to sea on a fishing trip, he would always give Euan the little carving, saying to him, "Keep *The Midnight Sun* safe for me, and I'll be safe home soon!"

And this time he'd added, "Keep it safe until Christmas – that's when I'll be back!"

So Euan kept the whalebone close, like a lucky charm, so that his father would return from the rough Arctic Ocean for the tree and Christmas dinner and the presents.

Now it was Christmas Eve, and Euan had only to keep the whalebone safe for a few more hours until his father came home.

"Let's light the candles on the tree, now," said Mother, louder than before, "and then when your father comes, he'll see them through the window."

But Euan still wasn't listening to her. His ears were filled with the heavy drumming of the sea, rolling and crashing over the rocks in the bay. He heard the wolf-howl of the wind – and through all this noise came the sound of a seal crying.

"There's snow on the way," Euan said to his mother. "Heavy snow."

"Are the seals telling you?" she asked.

"It's Oogruq. She's calling from the beach."

Euan's mother nodded. Although she couldn't understand the seals' cries herself, her son always seemed to know what they were saying.

He dreamed of the sea and loved the seals like brothers and sisters – especially Oogruq.

The year before, Euan had found a baby seal on the beach. She had a ripped flipper and was yelping in pain. He had fed her and bathed her wound until one day she had slipped into the waves, quite well again. Euan had watched the small seal go, hardly believing that she was big enough to swim across the endless ocean all the way to the Arctic and back. He had named her Oogruq, meaning *seal* in the language of the North. She would always call to him when she came to the beach. This time her cry warned him of danger out at sea.

Euan frowned. Oogruq was crying, "Danger! Snow!" Her voice was high and loud above the wolf-wind; she was warning him as loudly as she could. Euan knew the snowstorm was speeding towards the bay faster than a small fishing boat could travel over water. *The Midnight Sun* might be lost in the storm.

"Don't worry," Mother said, seeing her son's anxious face, "*The Midnight Sun* is nearly back. Daddy said so on the radio. He'll be in the bay before bedtime."

Euan hurried towards the door.

"Euan, where are you going?"
Mother asked.

"To the bay," he said, "to watch
for Daddy." Mother didn't stop
him. It was as if the sea was pulling
him towards it, so that he had to
go. She helped him into his outdoor
clothes, so thick, they made him
almost round. His legs looked short
and his hands in their thick gloves
were stumpy as flippers.

Out he went into the cold. Cold?
It was worse than cold. A snarling
wind bullied him as he pushed
against it over the stony path.
It was Christmas Eve. The air

should have been full of shimmer
and excitement. There should have
been carols round the Christmas tree
and the smell of roasting meat and
spicy pudding. But the storm didn't
understand that. It had ripped the
sea and the sky into little pieces and
was throwing them around in a wild
battle in the bay. No boat could
come through this in one piece.

Euan gripped the whalebone
tightly. "I'm keeping you safe," he
said, both to the carving and to his
father. "Please be safe!"

He knelt down on the rocky
shore near the harbour where the
boats pulled against their ropes,

tugged at by the tide. Oogruq was
high up the beach. Euan stretched
out his hand to her and she shuffled
to get close to him. The young seal
was pleased to see Euan and leaned
heavily against his legs. Then she
barked, telling of snow, storm,
sea-swell.

"My father's in danger," Euan said to her. "His boat is out there – and here comes the snow!"

Over the sea it swept, a white monster of a storm. It was so thick Euan couldn't see the sea at all.

"He won't be able to see the rocks!" Euan cried, thinking of the way his father always wove the boat in and out of the sharp rocks in the bay as he steered into harbour. Father knew the rocks almost as well as the seals did; he knew where each one lay and he knew its name. For the rocks all had names: Shark's Tooth, Splinter Rock, The Smasher. They waited to chew up boats thrown against them in a storm.

Euan showed Oogruq the whalebone with its carving of *The Midnight Sun*. Perhaps she could help him to stop the boat coming into the harbour somehow.

"What are you doing?" he shouted suddenly. The seal had taken the whalebone from his hand and before he could snatch it back, she had dived into the water.

"Come back!" he yelled. "I have to keep that safe. I have to keep my father safe!"

But Father wasn't safe now. No matter how hard Euan looked, he couldn't see the small seal.

How could she keep the whalebone in her mouth when she was rolled and rocked by such huge waves? The lucky charm wouldn't still be lucky if it fell to the bottom of the sea. He began to cry, the tears stinging his cheeks. He should never have come here alone. He should never have brought the whalebone with him, or shown it to Oogruq. She must have thought he was playing with her. She was too young to understand how important the whalebone was to him.

Then he saw something through his tears and through the shifting walls of snow. Thrown up and down on the plunging waves, there was a boat out in the bay. It tipped and tilted, pushed forward by the wind. Euan recognized it. It was the bravest boat ever. It was *The Midnight Sun* – and on it, though he was too far away to see, was Daddy. The boat was heading for Shark's Tooth, Splinter Rock, The Smasher. And in the blinding snow, his father couldn't see them; he wouldn't be able to steer the brave little boat and bring it safely into harbour.

"I've lost the whalebone!" he shouted to his father over the wind. "Go back! Don't come into the bay!"

His father was almost home, but the ship would be splintered and smashed. There was nothing he could do to help, and it was all his fault.

Great sobs burst from him that wouldn't stop. His voice sounded croaky and loud, a horrible, painful bark.

Then something was barking back. Above the drumming crash and roll of the sea and the wolf-howl of the wind, a seal was barking at him. This time it wasn't a danger call: it was the cry that Oogruq always made when she was coming to the beach.

Euan climbed up on to the harbour wall, clinging to a rope for safety. From here, he could see *The Midnight Sun* rising and falling. The rocks jutted their sharp teeth towards the little boat. Euan held his breath. But suddenly he caught sight of a shiny grey seal's head, like a silver light in the water. Oogruq swam first one way, then the other, weaving a path between the rocks, and Euan watched as *The Midnight Sun* followed. She was the eyes of the brave boat, guiding his father to safety.

Euan found himself crying again, but this time not from sadness. He felt so proud of the little seal. Eagerly, he watched the boat lurch into harbour, rescued from danger by Oogruq. Euan didn't know who to hug first as his father and the seal came to dry land. They were both part of his family and he loved them with all his heart.

In the stone house, the candles on the Christmas tree shone. It was Christmas Eve. Meat was roasting and the fire was warm. Father was carving the face of a large-eyed,

MALPAS
O 2/01/2010

fine-whiskered seal on the other side
of the whalebone, to remind
everyone who saw it that Oogruq
had saved *The Midnight Sun* from
being dashed on the rocks.

Euan opened the door of the
small stone cottage, and whispered
towards the bay. He needed to say
something before it was time to
open the Christmas presents.

"Happy Christmas, Oogruq, and
thank you for the best Christmas
gift of all!" he said, hoping she
could understand him.

And Oogruq, her voice full of
love, called back, "Happy Christmas,
Seal Brother."